My Day, Your Day

by Robin Ballard

Greenwillow Books
An Imprint of HarperCollins Publishers

For Sebastian

Pen and ink and watercolors
were used for the full-color art.
The text type is Futura.

My Day, Your Day
Copyright © 2001 by Robin Ballard
All rights reserved.
Printed in Hong Kong by South
China Printing Company (1988) Ltd.
www.harperchildrens.com

Library of Congress
Cataloging-in-Publication Data
Ballard, Robin.
My day, your day / by Robin Ballard
    p. cm.
"Greenwillow Books."
Summary: Children have a busy day
at day care while their parents have
a busy day at work.
ISBN 0-688-17796-4 (trade)
ISBN 0-06-029187-7 (lib. bdg.)
[1. Day care centers—Fiction.
2. Work—Fiction. 3. Day—Fiction.
4. Parent and child—Fiction.]
I. Title.   PZ7.B2125 Mv 2001
[E]—dc21   99-086462

10 9 8 7 6 5 4 3 2 1
First Edition

My day is at day care.

Your day is at work.

Bye-bye. See you later.

Building with blocks.

Planting seeds.

Circle time.

Reading.

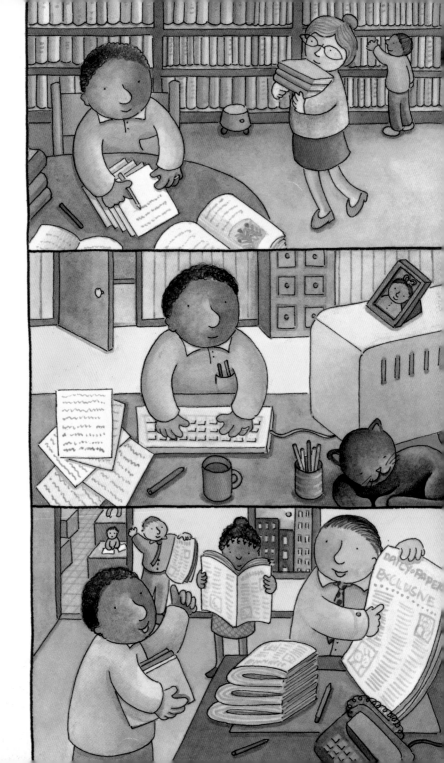

Playing outside.

Lunchtime.

Nap time.

In the bathroom.

Making pictures.

Working with trucks.

Hello, Mommy.

Hello, Daddy.

Let's go home.